ISBN: Softcover 978-1-5144-4962-2
EBook 978-1-5144-4961-5

Print information available on the last page

Rev. date: 01/09/2016

To order additional copies of this book, contact:
Xlibris
1-888-795-4274
www.Xlibris.com
Orders@Xlibris.com

MY LITTLE DRAGON LISSY

Lissy

Liz
Tess

Dee: My dragon is Lissy, and she is my very best friend, and I grew up loving her so much that I had to tell everyone about her. She is very colorful and very sweet, and she sings the dragon song all the time. I remember when I first met my Lissy. I was about five years old. She was the only thing around, and so was I, and I kept singing to myself, and it was the dragon song, and when I met Lissy, she was singing the dragon song too. So I asked Lissy, "How did you know the dragon song?" I have been singing it every day from the time that I could talk.

LISSY AND SHE SAID I KNOW THAT IS WHEN YOU STARTED SINGING IT SO WE COULD MEET EACH OTHER,

Dee: What do you mean?

Lissy: Well, when you started singing it, I started singing it too and know that you are older. I just sing it 'cause you do. So when I help young kids find their way, I sing the dragon song. Then they start singing it too. That is when I get to start helping the kids that need my help. We dragons don't live forever, but we do what we can, and that is what I am here for—the kids and you. Do you understand what I am saying?

Dee: Well, yes, I do, but I thought that you were just here for a limited time.

Lissy: No, I am here 'til I get the child on the right path and hope that the child will stay on that path.

Dee: Well, I sure am going to stay on the right path. But I love it when you come to see me.

Lissy: Well, all I can say about that is just always remember the song that we sing all the time, OK? I have to go for now, but I will be back very soon. OK, Dee?

Dee: Sure, but I hope that the child that you are going to help will be good to you 'cause you are the best friend that I have ever had and will ever have, and when I have kids, I want them to see you just like I do. OK, Lissy?

Lissy: Well, I hope that I will be around then.

Dee: What do you mean? You will be here for me, right?

Lissy: Well, like I said early on, we do not live forever.

Dee: I sure hope that you will be here longer than just a few years. I want my kids to see who you are too.

Lissy: Well, we can talk about this another time. OK, Dee? I have a child to help right now, so I will see you soon.

Dee: Gosh, I hope that she will be back soon 'cause I have no one to sing with when she is gone. I love my dragon song. Singing, singing, singing my dragon song. Singing, singing, singing it all day long. I really love my dragon, and we love to sing. So I'm singing, singing, singing my dragon song all alone. Just doesn't feel the same way if you had some one sing with you.

Lissy: I heard you singing the dragon song. Did you forget the words?

Dee: Yes, some of them, I did, sorry.

Lissy: It is OK. You are trying to get them right, huh?

Dee: Yes, but I just forgot some of them. Sorry.

Lissy: It is OK. When I am finished for the day, I will come back and teach them to you, OK?

Dee: Sure, Lissy. I think that would be great. You are just so cool, and I sure do love you, Lissy. You think you would like to take an adventure with me, Lissy?

Lissy: Maybe. Where do you want to go?

Dee: Far, far away . . . to when we first met. Can you remember back that far? I sure can.

Lissy: Well, I guess we can give it a try.

Dee: OK. Let's think back to when we were both younger, OK?

Lissy: Do you mean when you were younger or I was younger?

Dee: Both of us were younger. Can you go back that far?

Lissy: Sure, but getting back to this time might be a problem.

Dee: Why would that be a problem?

Lissy: It is just a little bit of magic can go a long way, that is all.

Dee: I was not talking about magic. I just wanted

to think back to when we were younger, that is all, when I first met you, Lissy.

Lissy: Let see . . . What were you, about five I think, and you were all alone and no one wanted to play with you. So you were just singing my song. And that was when I popped in on you. And you almost fell off the tree, and when you tried to get down, you got your foot caught, and I told you it was OK, I am a friend.

Dee: Yes, and you got me unstuck from the limb of the tree. And I asked who you were 'cause I could see your wings. And I thought that you were going to fall and so was I hoping that we would both be OK, and we were. I thought that you were just so cool and that I wanted you as my friend forever, and we have been ever since. I think that we have taught each other something to carry on in our days ahead.

Lissy: Yes, you thought that I was going to fall off the tree, and I thought that you were going to also.

Dee: Yes, we were both too high in the tree. To fall off it would have hurt me. So thank you so much for saving me back then. I sure care a lot about you, Lissy, and I have for a very long time.

Lissy: Well, I care about the kids that I help. But, Dee, you are the first kid that I have helped out off a tree, and I hope that I don't have any more kids in trees to help. That is a tight feat for a dragon like me. I have grown a lot through the years. And I mean grown wide, not up, and I am just a little bit older than you are, but I can fly, and we can help each other. When you need to go somewhere, I can fly you there on my back.

Dee: I have always liked riding on your back. It was so much fun, and we went places, and no one could see you. They just saw me in the air flying about. It was so much fun back then.

Lissy: We both might miss the days back then, but

we are still friends. Are we not? And we still do talk to each other, and I am here almost every day when I am not helping other kids.

Dee: I think that we need more time that we can spend together, if that is OK with you, Lissy.

Lissy: It would be OK, but I have so much to do with the kids that I help at this time. I am so sorry, Dee. Please don't be sad. I am still here.

Dee: I have just been thinking about when we went to so many places together and how much fun I had, that is all, and I just wonder can we ever do that again.

Lissy: Dee, don't worry, we can still go away like we did back then. It is just that it will have to be when I am not busy, that is all.

Dee: That would be so cool. Thanks, Lissy, that makes me happy. And it would be so cool to ride to places with you again 'cause you are the greatest dragon I have ever seen, well, the only dragon but still the best.

Lissy: Well, Dee, I have to go. I am changing colors, and it is a girl that needs my help.

Dee: OK, Lissy. I will see you again soon. Good luck.

Lissy: I will be back as soon as I can, Dee. Thank you so much. Just keep singing, I will hear you.

Dee: I will, and thank you so much. My dragon song, my dragon song, I sing about my dragon all day long 'cause I love my dragon song.

Lissy: Dee, I am back, and I have some good news for you. The little girl that I am helping is a friend of yours.

Dee: And who would that be? What is her name? Well, I don't think I know any real little kids, but I have a granddaughter, she knows a few of them.

Lissy: Well, I will tell you her name, but you cannot tell anyone that I said anything, OK?

Dee: Lissy, who would believe me?

Lissy: Well, you have a point there. No one can see me, except the ones who believe.

Dee: Yeah, you have a point there.

Lissy: Well, Dee, where do you wish to go tonight for our flight?

Dee: I just want to see the lights of the world, that is all. OK?

Lissy: Sure, we can do that. Just close your eyes, and we shall be on our way. Are you ready?

Dee: I sure am, and I have just thought that maybe I better get me a heavy jacket to wear.

Lissy: That is a great idea 'cause it is cold out here, and you need to be protected from the cold, OK?

Dee: Well, I am ready. Let's go.

Off we went into the wild blue yonder, and we are very high in the sky.

Lissy, it is just so pretty up here. I wish we never had to come down.

Lissy: Well, I have a lot of steam but not that much. Sorry.

Dee: No, I was just saying that I wish I never had to come down from here, that is all.

Lissy: Well, I wish that you could have your wish, but I have no idea of what to tell you. I know that you like being up high in the sky, but I have no idea what to do about that.

Dee: I think we will have a tree house when I get

the money to build one, when I see if I have enough trees.

Lissy: You know, I have an idea. We can build a ramp for the tree house when we build it so other people can come up and visit, even people in wheelchairs. Doesn't that sound great?

Dee: But that means that people will see what I have been dreaming of for years.

Lissy: Yes, that is just what you have been thinking about forever.

Dee: Yes, that is just great, and I think it will be great to have some of my friends over to my tree house. And I am going to build it big enough for a lot of people, and I want to have some great colors in it and pictures of you, Lissy, OK?

Lissy: Well, I have never had anyone take pictures of me for any reason, so why now?

Dee: Well, because you are so much fun, and I love you so much that I want everyone to see that I have a friend that means the world to me and this friend always will.

Lissy: You think of me as a friend? Why?

Dee: ’Cause you have always been there for me, and that is what I am going to tell them, and I don’t care if they think I am crazy ’cause you have always been here for me, and I will always be here for you, I hope.

Lissy: I think I will not mind if you have some pictures of me in your tree house. That would be fine to me, but what if people ask who I am?

Dee: That is fine. I will just tell them that I grew up seeing you and no one else could see you but me, and I will tell them that we have been friends for a very long time too.

Lissy: What if they ask if you can still see me?

Dee: Then I will tell them yes, all the time, and that will never change, I hope, anyway, 'cause you are always going to be my very best friend for now and forever.

Lissy: That is just so cool of you, and I thank you for saying that I have been your friend for so long. Dee, you will always be special to me too.

Dee: Well, thank you, Lissy. You are the dragon that stayed with me even when I was sick. you were there for me when I was in the hospital and when I came home, and I can't wait 'til my granddaughter can see you too.

Lissy: I hope that I will be here that long and meet your granddaughter, but will she be able to see me? That is the question.

Dee: What do you mean will she be able see you?

I can, and you are here for me. Why not her? She believes everything that Grandma tells her.

Lissy: OK, that sounds good to me. And I hope that she understands that I can be here and then I am gone, but she will be able to talk to me just like you do.

Dee: Wow! That is great, and there is one other thing—can she go for a ride when she gets to know you better too?

Lissy: We will figure that out when the time comes. OK, Dee?

Dee: That sounds very good to me, and thank you so much. Lissy, is there something wrong? You have been acting very strangely lately.

Lissy: Yes, I have something to tell you. I have two eggs that are going to be hatched very soon. And all I have to do is think of two names for them.

Dee: OK, what are they—girls or boys?

Lissy: Well, they are two girls, I hope, and they will hatch in just a few days. Then I can tell you for sure.

Dee: Wow! You have been keeping this from me all this time?

Lissy: Yes, and I am so sorry about that. I just thought that you would think that I was a bad dragon. But we have been talking about our lives, and so I just thought that I should do something about it, so I have two eggs about to hatch now, and that will make me feel better about living my life, and then they can take over where I left off.

Dee: What do you mean where you left off?

Lissy: Well, I mean, if I die before you, then I have someone to take my place. I will have the two babies to help me out.

Dee: I do see what you are saying. I have a

question—are you going to teach them our dragon song?

Lissy: Yes, I am, and they will know everything about all the kids that need help.

Dee: That is, like, so cool. You are sure the greatest, Lissy, and I will love you forever and beyond, and that is just wonderful. You are not just a dragon in my eyes, you are a star. And I think that the babies will be too.

Lissy: Well, if I have my way, you could try and teach them just like you did to me. Teach them our dragon song, I mean, the hip way.

Dee: That is the only way that I ever sing it—the hip way—'cause it is the cool way.

Lissy: Well, Dee, I have to go and see how my babies are doing. I am trying to think of names for them. They are both girls, and I need names.

Dee: How about Liz and Tess? That is good for

names, I think. What do you think about them? They sound great to me. But it is up to you and see if you like them.

Lissy: That sounds good to me, and I think that they will like them too.

Dee: Well, I am sorry it took me so long to think of names for them. But you did not say if they were girls or boys, so I was waiting to see, and that is the best that I could do, and I hope that they like their names too.

Lissy: I think that they will love their names—Liz and Tess. That makes me feel happy to see that they have names. It is great, and thank you so much, Dee.

Dee: Well, you asked for my help, and that is the best I could do for you. After all, we have been friends for a very long time, and I hope that we always will be 'cause you mean the world to me 'cause you are always here for me.

Lissy, you are a best friend to me too, and when I am sad, you talk to me and take me for a ride and cheer me up. Then I feel like someone does care about me, and it is you. You are always there, no matter what.

Lissy: Well, that is what friends are for.

Dee: And that is the best that I could do with the names for you too.

Lissy: The names are going to be great, and the girls will be flying very soon, and I will bring them by to see you in a few days, OK?

Dee: Oh, that would be so cool. And I just bet they are as sweet as you are.

Lissy: Yes, I will bring the babies by and see you tomorrow, but in the meantime, it is time for you to go and eat your dinner. And I will see you soon, OK, Dee?

Dee: OK, and thank you so much, Lissy. I sure

look forward to looking at the girls tomorrow, and you have a great night, Lissy.

Lissy: I will, and thank you for the names again.

Dee: You are more than welcome. Night.

Lissy: Night, Dee.

Dee: My dragon song, my dragon song, I like to sing it all night long.

My dragon song, my dragon song, I love to sing it all day long 'cause Lissy is the dragon I sing it for. That is why I sing it all day long. Lissy is special. Lissy is true. Lissy is a dragon for me and you. She is so special and so kind. She is a friend you can never find, not in human form anyway.

Lissy: Well, as I promised, I have brought you some cute babies to meet, Dee, and here they are Liz and Tess.

Dee: Oh, they look just like you when I met you way back when. So which one is which?

Lissy: That is up to you, OK, Dee?

Dee: Well, the one with the purple hair is Tess, and the pink is Liz, OK?

Lissy: That sounds great to me, and they just look up at us when we say the names to them.

Dee: Lissy, I am so glad that I have been a part of their lives on names and things that make me feel proud to be a part of their lives too. So are we going to teach them our dragon song too. Sure, so the kids will have it to call them for help. That is the only way that they will know when a child needs help—our dragon song.

Lissy: Well, Dee, you are right, and that is a big start. We need to teach them while we can, and while they are in one place together, that will make it easier for all of us.

Dee: My dragon song, my dragon song, I love to sing it all day long. I sing it high, I sing it low, it is with me here and wherever I go. My dragon song, my dragon song, how I love my dragon song.

Lissy: Come on, girls, sing it with us too.

Liz and Tess: OK, we will sing it too. Our dragon song, our dragon song, we will sing it all day long. We sing it high, and we sing it low, it is with us now and wherever we go. How did we do, Dee and Mommy?

Dee: You did just great, and I hope that you will like it as much as I do.

Liz and Tess: We love it.

Lissy: I see one of the babies' wings is changing colors. A child is in trouble, and I need to go with her. Dee, can you watch Tess for me for a few minutes, please?

Dee: Sure, I can, and we will just sing for a few minutes while you are gone, OK?

Lissy: Sure, and thank you so much.

Dee: You just show Liz how you work with the kids, and I will talk to Tess and see what she can show me, OK?

Lissy: Dee, that sounds great, and we shall be back very soon, and I will see what Tess can show me, what she can do while we are alone, and see what color her wings will turn when she is called. 'Cause when she is called, her wings turn different colors. That will tell me if it is a girl or a boy that Tess will be with. So if it is blue, she will help a boy. And if her wings turn pink or purple, it is a girl.

Dee: Wow! You are very well updated on what colors they turn when they have a child to help, huh?

Lissy: Well, that is what I do when I have a child to

see and take care of.

Dee: Wow! That is, like, so cool. Question—how big are they when they start taking the child for a ride on their backs like you did for me way back when? 'Cause I can't remember that far back anymore.

Lissy: Well, my girls just have to be about four months old. 'Cause dragons grow fast in the first few years, I think about four months, and the kids will be very pleased when they get to go for rides, and believe it or not, they never tell their mother or father when they do because it is when they are asleep, not while they are awake, Just like you did. But when you all get older, then you can ride for real, not when you are sleeping but when you are awake, and it is more fun when you can see something from flying.

Dee: I sure am happy that we are still friends and that I still go for a ride every now and then. I think we will be friends forever. And that is what I have always wanted, a friend forever, and that is you, Lissy.

Lissy: Wow! That is so kind of you, Dee. I think we have been friends for well over fifty years already, and I hope that we will be 'til it is the end of one of us, in other words, a long time still to come, we hope.

Dee: Wow! That is just way cool. I am so happy that we have each other.

Lissy: That is my wish for the both of us.

Dee: Tess is trying to talk to me, and that is so cool.

Lissy: What did she say? Or is she just playing around so you can hear her giggle? 'Cause that is what little Liz is doing too. They will not be talking 'til they are at least two months old, and that is about two weeks away. Wait just a minute.

Liz, what are you doing?

Liz: Mommy and Dee and Tess.

Lissy: Wow! I guess I was wrong. Liz is trying to talk.

Tess: Mommy.

Dee: Wow! I heard "Mommy" from Tess.

Lissy: Well, that means that they are well on their way to talking to the child that they are going to see and help.

Dee: Well, I think that they are so cute and that they are trying to grow up fast. And trying to talk this fast, what are they—just over a month old?

Lissy: Yes, they were hatched just a month ago, and they are in a hurry, I guess, but that is good, I think, and they can tell me what the child wants if they can't help the child themselves.

Dee: Well, I think that they take after their mom.

Lissy: What do you mean take after me?

Dee: Well, I remember when I was a young child and you came in to my life, and we were both singing my dragon song, and we have been friends ever since, and I have always been very happy for having you in my life, and there is not a day that goes by that I have ever had any regret.

Lissy: Dee, I have something to tell you, and I hate to do it.

Dee: What is it, Lissy?

Lissy: Well, I have something that I have on my mind that might hurt and that I have to do. I have been feeling bad, and I think that the end is near for me and that the girls will be taking over.

Dee: What do you mean feeling bad? You mean heartburn or something like that?

Lissy: No, it is not that. It is that I am forgetting

more than I remember lately, and that worries me. My girls are just too young to be left behind, and I would feel so bad, but I have you, Dee. You could help me with teaching the girls the right way.

Dee: Whatever you need, I can do, if I know what to look for, so I need your help, Lissy. Just tell me what I need to do, OK?

Lissy: Well, just make sure that the girls don't do something that they will be sorry for, OK?

Tess: Well, Mommy, I am going to see what this little girl needs, OK? My wings are turning blue and purple too. What is going on?

Lissy: That means that you have two little ones to see.

Tess: Way cool. Mommy, are you coming with me?

Lissy: Well, sure, I will go with you and see what you need to do, and I will stay away so they can't see me.

Tess: OK, Mommy, that is cool, and I will see what the kids need from me.

Lissy: That sounds great to me.

Liz: Dee, is my mommy OK? She is so tired all the time, and I think that there is something going on with her. Can you tell me what?

Dee: No, 'cause I have no idea what is going on as of yet 'cause she has not told me anything about how she feels.

Lissy: Well, I am back, and Tess is doing great. They are learning the dragon song.

Dee: You and I are the only ones that know the dragon song, Lissy. My dragon song, my dragon song, we all can sing my dragon song. My dragon goes here, my dragon goes there, my dragon will go most everywhere and singing my dragon song.

Tess and Liz: Mommy, we want to learn that song too, OK?

Lissy: Well, it is up to Dee. It is her song.

Dee: Well, it is OK with me as long as all of us are here together, that is all I ask.

Lissy: OK. As long as we are all together, we are doing just fine.

Dee: Can we talk without the girls?

Lissy: Sure. What is on your mind?

Dee: Well, you look like you are feeling better.

Lissy: Well, I am, and the girls are keeping me going. I think that I was just feeling bad 'cause the girls are growing so fast.

Dee: Yeah, Lissy, they do grow fast for the first year, just like kids do. But I have some news for you. I went to see my doctor, and she told me that I will be in a wheelchair for a long time, and I am not getting any younger.

Tess and Liz: We will be here for you, Dee, 'cause you are like our number 2 mommy, just without wings, that is all. You have been here for our mommy, so we will be here for you, just like you have been all this time for Mommy.

Lissy: Wow! That is great. My girls think of you as a second mommy, only no wings. Cool girls, huh?

Dee: What have you been telling your girls about me?

Lissy: Just that we met when you were very young, and so was I, and you were singing the dragon song, and that was what brought me to you—your singing.

Dee: Well, I sure am glad that we met, and I would not change all my tomorrows for the time that we have spent together, and I hope that we have a lot more time to spend together and the girls too.

Liz: You sound like you are going somewhere and we

are not going to see you much anymore, Mama Dee. Are you OK?

Dee: I am just fine, and that is just a statement, and that is all, I promise.

Tess: I like a promise ’cause that means that you will never leave us.

Lissy: Well, it just means that she is in no hurry to leave us.

Dee: Yes, girls, that is all it means, honest.

Tess: OK, we will believe you.

Liz: Yes, we do believe you . . . for now.

Lissy: What do you mean just for now? Is there something that we don’t know about that we should?

Dee: Not that I know of. I just know that I am getting old and I will not be here forever. I have cancer, and I am dying, but it will be a while. It is just the way that life is. I cannot tell when or where. It just happens.

Lissy: Yes, girls, that is all Dee can tell us for now. OK, you two just go and play for a few minutes while we talk.

Tess and Liz: OK. Mama Dee, we love you.

Dee: Well, girls, I love you both very much, and I always will.

Lissy: Well, we all need to go for a little fresh air so we can think. OK, all? Let's go.

Dee: OK, all, I will see you all later, OK?

Lissy: No, you are going with us, and we are going to have a great time, all of us together. Let's go.

Dee: I can't go. I have some things to do.

Lissy: No, you are going with us, so grab a jacket and a blanket, and you will be very warm.

Dee: So where are we going?

Lissy: You will see soon.

Dee: Are you keeping a secret on where we are going? Don't forget I am in a wheelchair, so I am limited on where I can go 'cause I can't walk very far.

Lissy: I do remember that, and so do the girls.

Dee: OK, well, let's go and get going on our way.

Liz: Where are we going?

Tess: Yes, Mommy, where are we going?

Lissy: You girls will see very soon. It is a place that Dee will recognize.

Dee: I will recognize the place that we are going to?

Lissy: Yes, you will 'cause it is where I first met you, Dee, and you were singing the dragon song for me. And I think that will be just great. I have not been there in a long time, and I thought that I would not see that place ever again 'cause I have moved on. And I can't do the traveling like I did before.

Lissy: What is going on? Are you OK?

Dee: Sure, I am fine. Are we ready to go and see what is going on in the world these days?

Lissy: Yes, we are all ready. Let's go, girls. Come on, Dee, climb up, and away we go.

Dee: This is so cool. I just love going on an outing with the girls, it makes me feel free.

Tess: Wow! Mommy, I think this is the best flight that we have ever been on. It is the farthest that we have ever gone before, and it is so sweet. I love it.

Liz: Yes, it is so cool way up here and so pretty, and

nobody can see us—that is the best part.

Lissy: OK, girls, we are going to land here and see what Dee can do here. It is her old home, and she is just too shocked to get down from here to see anything.

Dee: Well, I have seen enough. Can we go, please? It is just bad memories here, except when I met you, Lissy. That was the best time of my life, but can we go, please? I am feeling kind of out of sort.

Lissy: Sure, we can go now, and is there any place else that you would like to go?

Dee: No, I think it has been just a lot of fun just to come back to the old place, but I am feeling tired, and I need to rest, OK, girls?

Liz: Sure. We are tired too. That was a long way for us.

Tess: And it was so much fun we need to do it again sometime soon.

Lissy: Well, we are all back, and we are all tired, so we are all going to rest, OK?

Dee: Yes, and thank you so much for the ride, and I am very glad that we went there together, but now I have to lie down and rest. So I will see you girls tomorrow. Is that OK with you?

Tess and Liz: Yes, that is fine with us. We are going to play until we get a child's call. Night, Dee. We love you.

Lissy: Yes, Dee, you look like you need some rest, so you go and lie down, and we will see you soon, OK?

Dee: OK, I am going to sleep for a few minutes, so I will see you all soon. Night. Love you all.

Lissy: We need to keep an eye on Dee. I think there is something wrong with her, but I don't know what. She is always in a good mood, but today she wanted to go back to when we first met, and then there was a time that she could not remember the words to her own dragon song, but I do know when we get older, we have a space where we forget things, but I never thought that I would ever see her forget anything.

Dee: I am up and feeling great. My dragon song, my dragon song, I can sing it all day long. So come sing my dragon song.

EVERYBODY:

My dragon song,

My dragon song,

I love to sing my dragon song.

I could sing it all day long,

So come sing my dragon song.

I sing it by day,

I sing it by night,

I sing it alone with all my might.

I am singing it now

With sure delight,

It is my dragon song.

My dragon song,

My dragon song,

I love to sing it all day long.

I am here where I belong,

Just singing my dragon song.

(Repeat)

I hope that you all enjoyed this book, and I will write another as soon as I can, and no, I did not die. I just went for a visit to heaven, but I will be back with another book about Lissy, Liz, and Tess, but this is the end for now, so keep looking, OK?

This is . . .

THE END.

Edwards Brothers Malloy
Thorofare, NJ USA
September 2, 2016